For Andy

First Edition

ISBN: 0-316-46120-2

Library of Congress Catalog Card Number 90-53344
Library of Congress Cataloging-in-Publication information is available.

10 9 8 7 6 5 4 3 2 1

Printed in Hong Kong by South China Printing Company (1988) Ltd.

IT WAS JAKE!

Anita Jeram

Little, Brown and Company
Boston   Toronto   London

Danny has a very special friend, his dog, Jake.

Everywhere that Danny goes,

Jake goes too . . .

and he can do almost as many things as Danny.

One day, Danny was at home.

"I'm bored," he said.

Then he had an idea.

"I know," Danny said to Jake,

"let's dress up!"

Then Danny's mom came in. "Oh, what a mess!" she cried

when she saw the clothes all over the floor.

"It wasn't me, Mom," said Danny.

"It was **Jake !**"

"When you've cleaned up," said Danny's mom, "take Jake outside, and make sure you keep him out of trouble."

In the backyard

Danny had

another idea.

"I know," he said,

"let's dig for buried treasure!"

So he did.

He dug near the flowers . . .

He dug under the tree . . .

He dug everywhere.

But he didn't find

any buried treasure.

After a while, Danny's mom came out to look for him.

"Oh, look at my flowers!" she gasped. "What have you done?"

"It wasn't me, Mom," said Danny.

"It was **Jake !**"

"Go and get cleaned up right away,"

she shouted. "And take that

awful dog with you!"

In the bathroom

Danny said to Jake,

"If I have to have a wash,

I think you should

have one too."

But then Danny heard his mom coming.

"Mom . . ." said Danny.

"Look what Jake did!"

"Oh, no!" said his mom.

"If that dog misbehaves

once more, there will

be trouble!"

"Come on, Jake," Danny said. "Let's find something quiet to do."

Soon he was busy

cutting paper shapes.

"Now that's the last straw!" said Danny's mom

when she saw the paper everywhere.

"But it wasn't me, Mom," said Danny. "It was **Jake !**"

"Don't blame Jake!"

said his mom angrily.

"I think you must have made

all the mess because . . .

Jake can't use scissors . . .

and Jake can't turn on faucets . . .

and Jake can't hold a spade . . .

and Jake can't dress himself!"

"I'm sorry," said Danny. "I really am."

"I think you should say sorry to Jake!"

said Danny's mom.

"And you'd better give

him his supper now . . .

but you

can go

to bed

without

any."

Because Danny really was sorry for being bad

and for blaming everything on Jake, his mom brought him

a glass of milk and a sandwich anyway.

But while he was getting

ready for bed . . .

"That's funny," thought Danny,

"my sandwich has disappeared,

and I'm sure I didn't eat it.

But I think I know who did . . .

"It was **Jake !**"